KART COMP

BY ERIC STEVENS

ILLUSTRATED BY ABURTOV

STONE ARCH BOOKS
a capstone imprint

Jake Maddox books are published by Stone Arch Books
A Capstone Imprint
1710 Roe Crest Drive
North Mankato, Minnesota 56003
www.capstonepub.com

Library of Congress Cataloging-in-Publication Data

Maddox, Jake.
  Kart competition / by Jake Maddox ; text by Eric Stevens ; illustrated by
Jesus Aburto.
      p. cm. -- (Jake Maddox sports stories)
  Summary: Twelve-year-old friends Ted and Ashley are finally old enough
to go to Kart Kamp in the summer, where they meet Jake Stevens, son of a
famous driver, but soon Ted's competitive instincts start to get the better of
him, and camp becomes less about learning than winning.
  ISBN 978-1-4342-5976-9 (library binding) -- ISBN 978-1-4342-6209-7 (pbk.)
1. Karting--Juvenile fiction. 2. Competition (Psychology)--Juvenile fiction.
3. Best friends--Juvenile fiction. [1. Karting--Fiction. 2. Racing--Fiction. 3.
Competition (Psychology)--Fiction. 4. Best friends--Fiction. 5. Friendship-
-Fiction.] I. Stevens, Eric, 1974- II. Aburto, Jesus, ill. III. Title. IV. Series:
Maddox, Jake. Impact books. Jake Maddox sports story.
  PZ7.M25643Kaq 2013
  813.6--dc23

                              2012049364

Art Director: Bob Lentz
Graphic Designer: Veronica Scott
Production Specialist: Laura Manthe

Printed in the United States of America in Stevens Point, Wisconsin.
032013   007227WZF13

TABLE OF CONTENTS

CHAPTER 1

HOMETOWN HERO

Ted Forge leaned forward in his seat. Next to him, his best friend, Ashley Alvarez, did the same. They were watching the best event to visit their town all year: Indy car racing. Ted and Ash were both serious go-kart racers and racing fans. They had been looking forward to the race for months.

"I think Jeff has a real shot this year," Ted yelled. He had to shout to be heard over the roaring of the engines on the track.

Ashley nodded. They'd talked about Jeff Stevens a million times. He was their favorite driver, largely because he was from their town, Lakeville. He was having his best season ever this year.

The pack of cars sped by their seats and Ted and Ashley jumped to their feet. They cheered as Jeff's number-eight car zoomed across the finish line.

"Another first-place finish for hometown favorite Jeff Stevens!" the announcer called out over the loudspeaker. "That puts him just nine points out of first in the standings."

"One more win and he's got it," Ted said. He gave Ash a high five.

"Are you Jeff Stevens fans?" a boy next to them asked. He looked familiar.

Ash and Ted glanced at each other. "Isn't everyone here a Jeff Stevens fan?" Ted said.

"Yeah," Ashley added. "Jeff Stevens is from Lakeville, just like us."

"He's the hometown hero," Ted said. "You must not be from around here, huh? Otherwise you'd know that."

"Nope," the boy said, smiling. "I live in the city. My dad grew up here. We come up every summer for a few weeks."

Ted and Ash glanced at each other. They saw city kids come and go all the time in the summer. They came up to Lakeville to go fishing and boating and ride ATVs.

"I'm Jake, by the way," the boy said.

"I'm Ashley," Ash said, shaking his hand. "And this is Ted. We're the two biggest racing fans in Lakeville."

"In that case," Jake said, "I'll probably see you two tomorrow at Kart Kamp."

Ted raised his eyebrows. "You're going to Kart Kamp?" he asked.

Jake nodded. The Kart Kamp Racing, Engineering, and Pit School was going to be the highlight of Ted and Ash's summer. They'd spend the next two weeks speeding around the track in their own Indy-style go-karts. They'd learn driving techniques and even get a chance to work in the pit. Apparently they were also going to get two weeks with Jake.

"Great," said Ted, forcing a smile.

Ashley elbowed him in the side and motioned past Jake. She was grinning.

"What?" Ted asked.

"Look who's coming," Ash said.

Jeff Stevens was walking toward them. He was still wearing his racing jumpsuit and carrying his helmet under one arm.

Ted scrambled to find his racing program. "Do you have a pen?" he asked.

Ash already had her pen out. "Of course," she said.

Jake shook his head. "He's just a regular guy, you know," he said.

"Maybe you're not impressed, but we are," Ash said. "We have Lakeville pride."

"Yeah," Ted agreed. "Who do you root for, anyway? Is one of the drivers from down in the city?"

Jake stifled a laugh as Jeff walked up.

"Hi, kids," Jeff said. He clapped Ted and Jake on the shoulder. "Enjoy the race?"

"We sure did!" Ash said. She held out her pen. "Can you please sign my program?"

"Mine too?" Ted added, holding out his booklet.

Jeff laughed and took the pen from Ash. "Happy to," he said. Then he turned to Jake. "You ready to grab some lunch?"

"Yup, be there in a minute," Jake said.

Ted stared at Jake. Ashley's mouth dropped open.

"Okay," Jeff said. "Mom and I are ready when you are. See you kids later." With that, he walked off.

Ted and Ash stared at Jake. Jake smiled back at them.

"Jeff Stevens is my dad," Jake said. "Didn't I mention that?"

CHAPTER 2

KART CAMP

The next morning, Ashley and Ted arrived at Kart Kamp bright and early. Their friend Javier was waiting for them when they walked up.

"You two ready to race?" Javier asked.

"You know it," said Ted. "Let's check in so we can get on that track."

The Kart Kamp employees were manning desks set up inside. The man at the desk closest to the door waved them over.

"Morning, and welcome to Kamp," he said. "What are your names?"

The kids checked in and moved along the line of tables. They were given gloves, jumpsuits, helmets, and tools. At the last table, they chose the car they would use for the rest of Kart Kamp. The karts were smaller, less-powerful versions of the Indy cars driven by drivers like Jeff Stevens.

"Let's see," said the woman at the last table. "Ted Forge, number three. Ashley Alvarez, number four. And Javier Farmer, number five."

"I really wanted number eight," Ted said. He looked out the rear window at the track, where all the go-karts were parked.

"I don't even see a number eight," said Ash, peering over his shoulder.

"Yeah," said Javier. "I see one through seven, and I see nine through fifteen."

"Well, what happened to number eight?" Ted asked. "They wouldn't just skip it."

"Number eight is mine," Jake Stevens said as he walked up. He pointed over his shoulder out the front window. The three friends hurried over and looked out.

A trailer was delivering a brand-new, freshly painted go-kart. It looked just like Jeff Stevens's Indy car, only much smaller. A big number eight was painted on the side.

Ted's stomach twisted with jealousy. But when Ash and Javier ran outside to check out the car, Ted had no choice but to follow.

"Wow," said Ash.

"This is the coolest kart ever," said Javier, running a hand over the little chassis.

"Thanks," Jake said. "My dad had it specially made for Kart Kamp."

Ted crossed his arms and scowled at Jake. "Must be nice," he said. "I guess he got you that jumpsuit and helmet too?"

"Yup," said Jake. The jumpsuit he wore was identical to the one his dad had worn the day before. It even had the same two stickers at the top of the visor — one for each race Jeff Stevens had won that year.

Ted grabbed Ash and Javier by the wrists and pulled them aside.

"It's not fair," he grumbled.

"What isn't fair?" asked Javier. He was still staring at Jake's go-kart.

"Jake has an unfair advantage," Ted said. "He has a new car and gear. The rest of us have to use Kart Kamp's rental stuff."

"Maybe you're right," Javier said.

Suddenly the loudspeaker on the roof crackled. "Kart Kampers, please report to the track," a voice said.

"Well," said Ash, "I guess we're about to find out. It's time for the first race."

* * *

Sitting in his rental kart on the race track, Ted tightened his grip on the steering wheel. He could smell the gasoline from the karts in the air. The roar of the karts' four-stroke engines rumbled under his seat.

Jake's kart sat directly in front of Ted's. It was the only red car on the track. Jake's helmet was easy to see. It wasn't dirty and scuffed from being used. It was brand-new, shiny, and sleek with the number eight painted on both sides.

Ted swallowed hard as he stared at the start lights up ahead. The light flashed to green, and the track was filled with the sound of engines shrieking higher and louder as the karts took off.

Ted held tight to the steering wheel and stomped down on the accelerator. Ahead of him, Jake's kart pulled away from the pack.

He's ahead because his machine is better, Ted thought. *There's no way he got a quicker start on that green light than I did.*

It took all of Ted's upper-body strength to keep the car under control as he approached the first curve. For a little kart, it was sure powerful.

Up ahead, Jake's red kart sped into the first curve. Ted pushed harder on the gas pedal until his foot was flat on the floor.

Wait for it, Ted told himself going into the curve. *Don't brake too soon.*

At the last moment, Ted tapped the brake and cut hard to the left, passing Jake on the inside. But it wasn't enough. He was only in the lead for an instant before Jake sped around him.

It's just because Jake can race whenever he wants, Ted thought. *He probably has a dozen go-karts at home and his own personal track.*

The race was short — just four laps. Ted stayed close, but on the last turn Jake pulled away. He crossed the finish line and the checkered flag waved over him.

Ted came to a stop and hit the steering wheel in frustration. As he watched, Jake climbed out of his kart and put up his hands to celebrate his first win.

CHAPTER 3

WHO'S THE SNOB?

By the time they left the track for lunch, Ted's whole body was sore. It had been too long since he'd driven that much. He stood up and stretched his arms and legs.

When Ashley and Javier walked up, they headed inside to eat. They all grabbed slices of pizza and found seats at a long table.

"Good race," said Javier. He shook his head. "I can't believe how slow I was out there. My arms feel like jelly right now."

"We're just rusty," said Ted. "It's been a while since I drove like that."

Ashley laughed. "Rusty?" she repeated. "You were on Jake's tail the whole time!"

Ted shrugged, but he was happy to hear it. "Thanks," he said. He nodded at Ash. "You were pretty close to my tail too."

"For a few laps, maybe," Ash said.

"I would have passed Jake if it wasn't for that fancy kart," Ted said. "It's not fair."

Ash and Javier looked at each other.

"Maybe he's just a good driver, Ted," Javier suggested. "His dad sure is."

"That's another thing," Ted said. "He gets so much driving time. I bet his dad had a track built in their yard or something just for Jake to practice all the time."

Javier took a bite of his pizza. "That's probably not true," he said. "But yeah. He probably got more practice than we did most of the year."

Just then Jake walked up to their table, holding a paper plate stacked with pizza. "Do you mind if I sit with you guys?" he said. "I don't really know anyone yet."

Ted didn't answer. He just stared at his pizza and sighed.

Ashley elbowed him. "Sure," she said, smiling at Jake. She scooted over on the bench to make room for him. "Have a seat."

"Thanks," Jake said. He smiled gratefully and sat down, but hardly anyone spoke for the rest of lunch.

* * *

In the afternoons, Kart Kamp was all about classes. It wasn't like school, though. Instead, the classes were held outside in the garages or on the track itself.

For one class, they followed an instructor around the track on foot. He pointed out skid marks, scuff marks, and ideal places to brake, turn hard, and hit the gas.

By the time the last lesson was over, Ted was exhausted, but more excited than ever.

"The next two weeks are going to be amazing!" Ted said. He and Ashley were waiting for Ash's mother to pick them up.

"I know," said Ash. "I bet all our times improve a lot in the next race."

Ted watched as Jake stepped out from behind the building. He was walking with Javier. They were talking and laughing.

"Well, except for Jake's," said Ted. "He already has great gear, and he probably knows all the tips from his dad's coaches."

"Hey, guys," said Javier as he walked up.

Ted looked at Jake. "Is your dad's limo coming to pick you up?" he asked. "Or maybe the private chopper?" He regretted the words almost as soon as they left his mouth. But he couldn't stop himself.

Javier laughed. Ashley did not.

Jake didn't say anything. Shoving his hands in his pockets, he shuffled off and sat down on a bench to wait for his ride. Alone.

* * *

"That wasn't very nice," Ash said as they sat in her mom's car on their way home.

"What?" Ted asked.

"You were rude to Jake," Ash said quietly.

"Oh, please," said Ted, rolling his eyes. "He didn't even care. He's just a snob."

Ash crossed her arms and stared out her window. "I think *you're* the snob," she said.

CHAPTER 4

DESPERATE TO WIN

The next morning at Kart Kamp, the kids met on the track. They were all suited up with their helmets under their arms. Their karts were parked along the track.

"Today we'll practice mastering the line," the driving coach announced. "Try to remember what we talked about yesterday. Brake at the right time, cut the wheel at the right time, and keep your foot down on the straights and wide curves."

He scanned the group of eager faces. "One more thing," he said. "This morning is just a practice. This is not a race."

Ted glanced across the group and found Jake. Jake was staring right back at him.

"Helmets on. Get in your karts," the coach said. "I'll tell you when to start. And remember, no racing."

Ash bumped Ted with her shoulder as she walked passed him toward her kart. "I hope you were listening," she said.

"Yeah, yeah," said Ted. He grabbed his helmet and climbed into his kart. He clicked the ignition and pulled onto the track.

Ted rolled into line right behind Jake's shiny red kart. Before long, every kart was on the track, weaving back and forth on a slow lap around the track.

As Jake's car reached the start line, the driving coach pointed at him. The coach lowered the green flag and Jake floored it. His kart zoomed away from the pack.

Ted gripped his wheel tightly as he rolled along helplessly. "Come on," he muttered, staring at the coach. "Start me already."

It seemed like ages, but the green flag finally came down again. Ted stomped on the accelerator, making his wheels squeal. He zipped into the first curve and looked ahead on the track. Jake was already on the first straightaway.

Ted kept his eyes on every turn, doing his best to remember the line the coach taught him the day before.

When he reached the straightaway, Jake was already heading into the next turn.

I have to catch him, Ted thought. That meant keeping his foot down on the accelerator as long as possible and braking as late as he could.

The first two turns, he got the timing just right. At the end of the first lap, Ted had almost managed to close the gap between himself and Jake. But it wasn't enough.

All fifteen karts were spaced around the track now like the coach had wanted. Ted spotted Javier's kart, number five, at the very back. He was in last place, right in front of Jake. And he was slowing down.

Ted smiled. He knew what Javier was doing. He was going to box Jake in so Ted could catch up. Jake came up behind Javier and zipped back and forth, trying to pass. But Javier refused to let him go around.

This is my chance! Ted thought. He hit the straightaway a hundred feet behind Jake and Javier. His foot was heavy on the gas.

Jake couldn't keep his foot down. Javier wouldn't let him get that fast. Before long, Ted had cut the lead in half.

It was working!

Just as Ted caught up with Jake, Javier slipped to the outside of the track. Ted zoomed past both cars on the inside. He was going to win!

Up ahead, the driving coach stood in the infield. He waved the black flag furiously. Ted and Javier were in big trouble.

CHAPTER 5

BENCHED

"I tried to warn you," Ash said. Ted and Javier slumped on the bench behind the camp building. From there, they could see the track, but they weren't allowed on it.

"I know," Ted said miserably.

The black flag meant Ted and Javier had to pull off the track for unsportsmanlike conduct. They both got a big lecture about driving safety, and about how practice drives were not races.

After lunch and mechanics lessons, everyone else was going down to the track for a race. But the boys had to sit there on the bench.

"Well," Ash said. "Enjoy the race." She pulled on her helmet and shook her head. Then she turned and walked to the track.

* * *

"I hope you're happy," Ash said in the car on the way home.

"I'm not," said Ted. He crossed his arms.

"You know you missed three hours of driving today," Ash said.

"I know," said Ted.

"That's three hours of practice," Ash said. "Three hours you could have spent actually improving as a driver."

"I know!" Ted snapped.

"All because you were trying to beat Jake," Ash said, "a boy you hardly even know. A boy who hasn't done anything to you."

Ted rolled his eyes.

"It's true," Ash said.

Ted shrugged and looked out the window as the car pulled into town. He didn't want to admit it, but maybe Ashley was right.

CHAPTER 6

AN UNFAIR ADVANTAGE

"I'm going to be nicer to Jake today," Ted said when Ash climbed into the front seat of his dad's pickup.

"I'll believe that when I see it," Ash said.

Something was blocking the driveway to Kart Kamp when they pulled up. Ted and Ashley leaned forward to get a better look.

"What is that?" Ashley asked.

"It looks like Jeff Stevens's car," Ted said. "With a trailer on the back."

Ted and Ash had never seen Jeff's car up close, but they'd both read tons of articles about it and watched road-test videos online. The make and model was on both of their lists of dream cars.

Ted's dad pulled into the drop-off circle. "Have a fun day," he said.

Ted and Ash hopped out and joined a small group of campers who'd gathered around the car and trailer.

Jake climbed out of the passenger seat and walked to the trailer. The campers gasped when his dad opened the door.

"Hey, kids," Jeff said, getting out of the car. "Excited to do some driving today?"

He opened the trailer door and pulled out the ramp. Jake's red go-kart rolled out and onto the gravel.

"Thanks, Dad," Jake said.

"No problem," his dad replied. He closed up the trailer and climbed back into the car, waving as he drove off.

Ted stepped up next to Jake. "You bring your kart home every day?" he asked.

"No," said Jake, pushing the kart toward the track. "It needed a tune-up."

"So you had your dad's pit team do it?" Ted said, shaking his head. "I can't believe this guy!"

"Ted," Ashley said. "Stop it."

"This is so unfair!" Ted shouted, ignoring Ash's warning. "He has all the best gear, and he can practice whenever he wants. And on top of that, he has his dad's crew tuning up his kart."

Jake stopped pushing his kart and turned to face Ted. He didn't say anything.

"We're supposed to be learning how to tune up our own karts," Ted went on. "It's half the point of the camp. It's not just about showing off how cool your dad is and how much money you have!"

Jake took a deep breath. "Look," he said. "I have another go-kart at home in the garage. It's just as good as this one. You can use it all summer if you want."

"What?" Ted said.

"And I can ask my dad's team to help you as much as they can," Jake offered.

Ted felt his face get hot. He glared at Jake. "That's not the point!" he snapped. "I don't need your help!" With that, Ted stomped off toward the track.

Ash caught up with Ted at the track. "What is your problem?" she demanded.

"Oh, leave me alone," Ted said. He pretended to be concentrating hard on his car. He really didn't want a lecture from Ash — mainly because he knew she was right.

"I will not leave you alone," Ash said. "You say it's unfair and treat Jake like dirt. Jake offers to level the playing field for you, and you shout at him some more."

"Why are you defending him so much, anyway?" Ted said. He squinted up at her. "You have a crush on him or something?"

A few of the guys nearby laughed, and Ted smiled.

"Shut up, Ted," Ash said. Her face went beet red, and she hurried away.

"I'll take that as a yes," said a boy nearby. The rest of the guys chuckled.

Now I'm insulting my friends too? Ted thought. *What is wrong with me?*

CHAPTER 7

LEVELING THE PLAYING FIELD

Ted managed to avoid Ashley for the rest of the day. The next morning, as his dad drove them both to camp, Ted kept his eyes on his hands and knees.

At lunch, Ted finally got up the courage to talk to Jake. He found him sitting at a table by himself.

"Hi," Ted said. "Can I sit here?"

Jake shrugged, so Ted sat down.

"Listen," Ted said. "I'm sorry about yesterday. I shouldn't have shouted at you."

"It's okay," Jake said.

"And I'm sorry for the day before that too," added Ted. "And before that."

Jake laughed. "It's okay," he said. "Besides, you're right."

Ted's eyes shot open. "I am?" he said.

Jake nodded. "As of today, I'm using a Kart Kamp go-kart," he said. "I got the last one, obviously. It is number eight, though."

"Fair enough," Ted said.

"My dad thinks I'm nuts," Jake said. "He says they use every advantage they can in the pros."

Ted opened his drink. "Maybe he's right," he said.

"But in the pro leagues, they're a team," Jake said. "They take the advantages their sponsors give them. My dad isn't supposed to be my sponsor."

"True," Ted said.

"I didn't get any of these advantages on my own," Jake said. "My dad just handed them to me."

Ted took a long drink. "So no hard feelings?" he asked.

Jake shook his head. "No," he said. "But I'm still going to whoop you on the track."

Ted laughed. "We'll see about that," he said. "We'll see about that."

CHAPTER 8

GOOD-NATURED RIVALS

Ted and Jake spent the next several days as good-natured rivals. On and off the track, they competed over everything. But they had fun anyway.

In mechanics class, they had races to see who could disassemble the rear axle and shocks the fastest. During their warm-up exercises, each tried to do more sit-ups and more push-ups than the other. When they jogged the infield, their laps always ended with sprints for the finish line.

On the third-to-last day, the driving coach gathered the campers together before they headed home for the night.

"All right, drivers," he said. "We're nearing the end of your two weeks at Kart Kamp."

"Aww," the campers said all together. Everyone looked disappointed.

The driving coach smiled. "Tomorrow is a big day," he went on. "In the morning, we'll review everything you've learned over the past eight days. And then in the afternoon, it's qualifier time."

The campers cheered. The qualifiers would determine what position each camper's karts would start from in the Kart Kamp Grand Prix. The big race was going to be held on Friday, the last day of camp.

"The qualifier will be held in three stages, just like in the pro league," the coach explained. "The winner of the last stage will be at the pole."

Ted and Jake looked at each other and smiled. It was finally time for a real race.

CHAPTER 9

RACING FOR THE FINISH LINE

On the second-to-last day of Kart Kamp, the driving coach walked the campers around the track. He pointed out when they should keep the gas pedal flat to the floor and where they should let up. He explained when to brake and how hard.

In engineering, the mechanics teachers reminded them what to check before the race. They showed them again how to tighten this, and adjust that.

Jake and Ted hardly heard a word. All they could think about was the qualifier. They couldn't wait to get behind the wheel and show their stuff on the track.

At lunch, everyone was too excited. Finally, the driving coach blew his whistle.

"Time for the first stage!" he shouted. The campers cheered and ran to the track and their karts.

* * *

Before long, the sound of fifteen revving go-kart engines filled the air. The driving coach dropped the green flag. The cars blasted off.

For twenty minutes, every camper did his or her best to master the course. They had to get every turn, every brake, and every straightaway just right.

Ted gripped the wheel and peered over the windshield as a curve as it approached. Every second counted in qualifiers.

Ahead of him, he spotted kart number eight, Jake's car. But he had to ignore it. He'd get his chance to compete with Jake tomorrow. Today he was racing against the clock and himself.

After the twenty minutes were up, the driving coach waved the caution flag. Everyone pulled to the side and parked. They climbed out of their karts and gathered around the coach.

"Great job out there, everyone," he said. "But as you know, only some of you will move on to the next stage. Karts two, three, four, eight, eleven, and thirteen will move forward. The rest of you will be in the back of the grid."

There was some cheering — especially from Ted, Ash, and Jake — and some groaning — especially from Javier.

"Get ready for the second stage, drivers," the coach said.

"Good job, guys," said Javier. "Hey, Ted. If you need any help blocking this one out, I'll hang back a little in the Grand Prix."

"Hey!" Ash said, and the boys laughed.

"He's kidding, Ash," Ted said. "We won't do anything like that again."

Ash was eliminated in the next stage. In stage three, Jake, Ted, and a third driver competed for pole, second, and third positions. Jake came in second, and Ted took third. Even so, Ted was smiling.

* * *

"Kart Kamp has been a lot more fun since you and Jake started getting along," Ash told him on the way home.

"Yeah," Ted agreed. "Did you see him spin out on his last lap in stage three?"

Ash laughed. "He said he's still getting used to the camp's kart," she said.

"Maybe," said Ted. "I think he was just pushing too hard around that last curve. It was a pretty sweet spinout, though."

"Nervous?" Ash said. "For tomorrow, I mean."

"Nah," said Ted. And he wasn't. He was just excited.

CHAPTER 10

A SURPRISE WIN

The next morning, the campers suited up for the Grand Prix race. As they walked down to the track to meet their karts their parents cheered from the stands.

As the announcer explained the race to the spectators in the stands, the driving coach stepped up to the waiting campers.

"We have a surprise today," he said. "We've switched around your numbers."

"But we're used to our karts!" Ted said.

The coach smiled. "That's what you think," he said. "We've been switching the numbers every night. Some of you haven't driven the same kart twice."

"Unbelievable," said Jake.

"Today, you'll drive a random kart," the coach said. "Only the referees and timekeepers will know who's in which kart."

"Why the switch?" Javier asked.

"We want you to understand that it's not personal on the track," the coach said. "It's racing. You should be focused on giving it your best, driving the right line, taking the turns just right. You should be focused on your own driving, not your competition."

Ted smiled at Jake. It made sense to them.

* * *

Ted climbed into his kart. He tried to figure out who was where, but he couldn't see the rest of the pack lined up behind him.

The cars started around the track toward the rolling start. As the first car's wheels hit the start line, the drive coach dropped the green flag. They were off.

Ted cleared his mind. He didn't think about competing with Jake. He didn't think about how good his gear was, or which kart he'd ended up in. He didn't even think about lines or when to brake. He just drove like it was second nature.

Ted slipped around the pole kart on the turn, slid to the inside, and jumped into first place. On the straightaway, he could sense the second kart — whosever it was — right behind him.

Ted focused on the track and his kart. At the turn, he held his foot down till the last moment. Then he hit the brake hard and cut the wheel, holding onto the inside line.

As he came tight around the bend, the second-place car slid around the outside, speeding up until they were neck and neck.

Ted risked a glance at the driver. But with the scuffed white helmet and tinted visor, he couldn't tell who it was.

Both drivers slowed down for the hairpin curve coming up. Ted jockeyed for the inside, but the other driver shot around the outside, and cut in front of him.

At the next straight, Ted punched the gas hard. The rest of the pack was right behind him. He wondered how Ashley and Javier were doing.

Huh, he thought. *I don't even know if this is Jake in front of me.* But he assumed it was.

The karts reached a long series of slight curves. Getting the right line and staying on the gas was the rule for this section.

Ted gripped the wheel and pushed the gas pedal to the floor. On the second little curve, he pulled ahead of the other kart. For an instant, he had the lead. But at the next curve, they were neck and neck again.

They stayed tight around the final bend. From behind, a third driver jockeyed for the lead. The third kart took the bend wide and slid between Ted and the first-place kart, sending Ted back into third place.

Ted thumped his steering wheel. Then he took a deep breath. *Focus*, he thought. *Focus on the driving, not on the other karts.*

* * *

Ted stayed at the front of the pack nearly the whole race. He had no idea who his top competitors were, but he assumed Jake was one of them.

On the final lap, Ted saw his chance. He kept his foot down and drifted to the outside. He slipped past the second car and moved up on the first-place car's tail.

But as they straightened out, Ted lost control, just for a fraction of a second. His kart wobbled and he slipped back to third.

It was all he could do on the final straight to bring his kart neck and neck with the second-place car. As the checkered flag fell, he was tied for second.

Ted pulled off to the side and watched as car number eight took a victory lap.

Climbing out of his car, Ted took off his helmet. The driver of the car he'd tied with climbed out too.

"Jake!" Ted said as the other driver pulled off his helmet.

"Great race, Ted," said Jake. The boys shook hands. "So who was that?"

Ted shrugged. "I don't know," he said.

Javier walked over. "I think I know who it is," he said. He pointed at the stands, where three people were still on their feet cheering: Ted's parents and Ashley's mother.

"No way," said Ted.

Kart eight finished its victory lap and pulled over next to them. The driver pulled off her helmet, a big smile on her face.

"Nice race, boys," Ashley said. "Better luck next summer."

AUTHOR BIO

Eric Stevens lives in St. Paul, Minnesota. He is studying to become a middle-school English teacher. Some of his favorite things include pizza, playing video games, watching cooking shows on TV, riding his bike, and trying new restaurants. Some of his least favorite things include olives and shoveling snow.

ILLUSTRATOR BIO

Aburtov has worked in the comic book industry for more than 11 years. In that time, he has illustrated popular characters like Wolverine, Iron Man, Blade, and the Punisher. He lives in Monterrey, Mexico, with his daughter, Ilka, and his beloved wife.

GLOSSARY

caution (KAW-shun) — carefulness or watchfulness

competition (kom-puh-TISH-uhn) — a contest of some kind

familiar (fuh-MIL-yur) — well-known or easily recognized

identical (eye-DEN-ti-kuhl) — exactly alike

qualifiers (KWAHL-uh-fye-urz) — a preliminary contest

spectators (SPEK-tay-turz) — people who are watching an event but not participating in it

technique (tek-NEEK) — a method or way of doing something that requires skill, as in the arts, sports, or the sciences

DISCUSSION QUESTIONS

1. Jake's dad was a famous driver. Was it unfair for Jake to go to Kart Kamp? Talk about your opinion.

2. Why do you think Ted was so angry with Jake from the start? Discuss some possible reasons.

3. Were you surprised by the ending of this book? Who did you expect to win the race?

WRITING PROMPTS

1. Pretend you're in Jake's position. Would you have used the kart your dad made for you? Write about why or why not.

2. What do you think is the hardest part of kart racing? What do you think is the best part? Write a paragraph about each.

3. Do you think Ted was a bully in this book? Write about some other ways he could have reacted to Jake's arrival at Kart Kamp.

KARTING HISTORY

The first kart was invented in 1956 by Art Ingels, an employee of a American race-car company. He used a lawnmower engine to build his kart. When Ingels demonstrated his kart, another American, Duffy Livingstone, saw it and decided to build his own. Soon, the first kart races were being held in the Rose Bowl parking lot in Pasadena, California.

In 1957, the first official rule book was written by the International Karting Federation in California. After this, karting spread rapidly across the United States. American airmen later brought the sport to the United Kingdom, and by 1962 there were karting clubs all over the world.

KARTING EQUIPMENT

It's important to wear the proper safety gear whenever you're karting to protect your hands, head, and body. You should never go out on your kart without wearing the proper equipment:

- **helmet** — buy a helmet that fits snugly so it can't be pushed off when fastened

- **racesuit** — designed to protect your body if you accidentally fall out of your kart

- **gloves** — buy strong gloves to prevent blisters and keep your hands from slipping

- **boots** — must cover and protect your ankles from knocking around

- **earplugs** — wear earplugs whenever you're driving to protect your ears from all the noise